ALAN GEOFFRION
BROKENTRAIL

ALAN GEOFFRION

A NOVEL

BROKENTRAIL

NOW AN AMC ORIGINAL MOVIE

FULCRUM PUBLISHING
GOLDEN, COLORADO

ISBN-13: 978-0-7394-7031-2
ISBN-10: 0-7394-7031-0

Printed in the United States of America

Editorial: Sam Scinta, Katie Raymond
Book layout and design: Jack Lenzo
Cover image courtesy of AMC
Mandala images copyright © Olga Vasilkova/Dreamstime.com

Fulcrum Publishing
16100 Table Mountain Parkway, Suite 300
Golden, Colorado 80403

For Danielle and Donald

PROLOGUE

The little stallion turned his head into the wind, gently flared his nostrils, and inhaled the night air. He smelled the budding sage, the thawing earth, and the faintest hint of the scent of carnivores. Clouds scudded past a waning moon. Spring had come early to the mesa, and with it the rhythms of the changing seasons. Wolves ventured south, vying with the coyotes for the pronghorn fawns and any early foals on the Owyhee Range. Spring stirred the young colts, emboldened with hopes of having mares that would be coming into heat. This would be the stallion's ninth year on the range. He had covered this band of mares for the last four seasons, protecting it from predators and colts eager to challenge his claim. He was acutely aware of the world around him. It was all encoded deep inside him as it had been in his sire and all the other stallions going back to the little Spanish horses that swam ashore from the galleons off the shores of Hispaniola almost four hundred years before.

◎ ◎ ◎

A sorrel mare, heavy with foal, had been up and down for hours, positioning the unborn inside her. The sounds of her labor and the smell of her afterbirth would soon be on the night air. Again he breathed in the night, deep into his synapse. The air was thick with the smell of the sage that the horses had trampled on. The buttery moonlight shone on his spring coat. He quietly moved out into the darkness, feeling a nagging twinge in his hock. In the darkness out beyond the band of mares, he pawed the earth and snorted loudly to the seen and the unseen.

A flat gray line of morning fog and smoke from cook fires hung evenly over the village. The damp morning air awakened the timeless scent of a thousand years of dust and dehydrated animal and human waste. The nameless village lay in a nameless part of the western Guandong Province of China. Mud huts surrounded a compound of deteriorating walls. Inside the walls gathered people as dreary and desperate-looking as the land they lived in. The village headman watched as his verdict on the man who knelt before him was carried out. Roosters scratched and pecked at the litter on the ground. A cord tied fast around the man's thumb was pulled as two men held the wretch and forced his hand on a stump. The headman nodded and a third helper dropped the axe, severing the hand from its shaking owner. The villagers looked on in silence. Poverty had long ago ground away all their emotions. Their presence was merely a requirement, much as was their daily toiling in the fields of a thankless land. A woman sobbed as three children clutched about her. Her anguish was as much for what her future held as for the wretch whose bloody hand lay before them.

The sergeant major strutted up the middle of the dirt road, which was lined with a dozen tin-roofed buildings. Lydesdorp had been the provincial capital of northern Transvaal. Swagger stick held under his left arm, his boots powdered with dust, he marched toward a detail of soldiers.

The men were using mules to drag dead horses beyond the village. It was an hour before sunset, and still the sky was filled with soaring vultures. They glided in big, looping circles on thermals that rose from the African bushveld.

By the time the sergeant major caught up with the working detail, they had just removed the rope from around the ankles of a stout dun. The gelding lay with a distended belly, stiff legs, and its mouth open on its side next to a pile of thirty or so dead horses.

A soldier knelt beside the animal and brushed the horse's dark forelock to the side of its face. Its big, beautiful dark eye stared at nothing. The soldier turned his head at the sound of the sergeant major's footsteps.

"Cramer, no time to be sitting on your haunches. I want this mess cleared up before retreat," said the big Yorkshireman, pointing to the carcass with the swagger stick. "There's nothing you can do for them now, laddy. They've served their purpose," he said, tucking the stick back under his arm.

"You mean Lord Kitchner's. There must be three thousand dead 'tween here and Fort Edwards. They say Kitchner's lost two hundred thousand horses, and he still can't catch the Dutchmen," said the soldier as he rose and wiped his hand on his trousers.

"Steady on there, boy'o. Talk like that will get you in front of the provost. Aye, he's a wee one," said the sergeant major, nodding to the dun.

"He's a mustang, sergeant," said the soldier in a low voice.

"What's that, soldier? Speak up," snapped the sergeant major.

The soldier straightened and in a clear voice said, "He's a mustang, sergeant major. From America."

"From America? Ah, well. Carry on."

CHAPTER ONE

Print Ritter had to quit. His body knew it even before he did. The imperceptible pains worked to slow his steps across the ground and the aches spoke to him as he sat astride a horse. He refused to see it that way, but it was the truth. He adhered to the old saw that "it was better to wear out than rust out."

He removed his hat and wiped his brow. From above his eyebrows, his forehead was as white as a fish's under-belly; below, the look and color of tobacco. His white moustache drooped to his jaw. He ran his fingers through his silver hair before he replaced his hat. He had a paunch, but that was it. He carried no extra weight. His clothes were worn but tidy. He squeezed his wiry legs and the big chestnut moved out at a ground-eating trot.

Long flying wedges of Canada geese passed overhead, and wherever there was water, it was covered with pintails, most of them with their heads underwater and their pointy little asses in the air. Spring was sure coming early this year, he thought. And that made him think of empty stock tanks and dry creek beds. It seemed to him that early springs meant waterless summers. Then again, maybe not. He was about halfway from the OO Ranch, heading to the Gap Ranch in the northern corner of Harney County. Those honkers will make it there before I do, he thought. The waterbirds had converged on Silver Lake, resting on their journey up to Canada and on to the Arctic Circle.

It was just north of the lake that the war chief Buffalo

Horn had met his maker during the Indian Wars in eastern Oregon. Print had been working for the cattleman Peter French back in the summer of '78. He had been hired on to "sort out" young colts, but he was up for any chore Mr. French assigned to him. The two had struck it off from the first time they met. Print liked the way Peter French handled his men and his cows, and French liked the way Print finished off his horses. They and about a dozen hands were working over on the Diamond Ranch, branding, when Coon Smith raced in yelling that "about twenty-five" mounted braves were heading for the branding camp. It had been at the Diamond Ranch that a band of Bannocks had earlier on burned out George Smyth and his son, forcing them with intense barrage from their repeating rifles back into their cabin, where father and son burned to death. From then on, everyone got anxious anytime there was a sighting of two or more Indians in the countryside.

French, being the only one armed at the time, ordered all the hands to make a run for it back to the P Ranch. They threw the Chinaman, their cook, up on a horse and made a straight line for the P. French took up a position and started taking potshots at the approaching band. When they got close, he took off until he found a new position that offered some cover, and started dropping more of them as they advanced. He continued this until his men were over the trail crossing at McCoy Creek and the Bannocks felt that he was taking all the fun out of their day. The Chinaman had not lasted long on the galloping horse and had fallen off. The band caught the cook and put him to a gruesome death so that their entire day was not a loss.

Later, Print and Peter French and other cowhands joined up with a Colonel Bernard and made a fight of it at Silver Lake with the joined forces of Bannocks and Paiutes under Buffalo Horn. French had said that "it wasn't required and it was strictly on a volunteer basis." Print didn't care one way or the other. He went because Peter French had asked. It wasn't because of the Bannocks and Paiutes, or the Chinaman, or old man George Smyth and his son who got roasted in their cabin. He had left that kind of thinking a lifetime ago, back in the Valley Campaign, chasing Phil Sheridan up and down the Shenandoah. He went because this man he considered a friend had asked.

In the end, four troopers were killed and nearly fifty braves, including Buffalo Horn. He had been a handsome devil, even in death, thought Print. And a crafty one too. He had convinced the governor to give his braves more guns and ammunition so they could hunt for themselves, as the beef allotments from the government weren't enough to live on. Politicians. Worse than lawyers. Skimming money from the government beef fund, then allowing the tribes to arm themselves so that they could go out and kill ranchers trying to raise enough cows to feed the country, including the Indians. Print spat.

And now at his stopover at the OO Ranch, he learned from the Hanleys that his old friend Peter French had been murdered. They said it was over cows. There ain't enough cows in Christendom to be worth getting killed over, thought Print. But then maybe it wasn't really about cows. Maybe cows were just an excuse, and there was another issue. And there were issues in life worth making a stand over. They said that the fella that had done it was indicted by a coroner's jury that had been convened at the Sod House spread. Due to a low-set bail, and a firm of brass-buttoned lawyers all the way from Portland, the culprit ducked out of the justice he deserved. Politicians and lawyers. Print spat again. Forget it. Push on. Follow the honkers, the pintails, and terns north.

The following morning, the sun rose on his right. The clumps of manzanita cast long shadows across the range floor. The day would warm up quickly. Definitely an early spring, he thought. The waterbirds were high in the sky, winging north. A frantic jackrabbit darted left, then right, and disappeared into the brush. He had been in the saddle since before first light. He was betting he could make his destination before breakfast was over. He hadn't wanted to waste time making a fire, not even for coffee. He liked riding at this time of the day, especially when the weather was good. He could always have coffee, but not good weather.

He pushed Bob Tate into a lope as he sighted the Gap Ranch compound. A half an hour later, as he eased the big chestnut up at the approach to the ranch quarters, a spry man stepped off the porch to meet him.

"I'm lookin' for a Tom Harte," said Print.

The spry man said nothing. Print took his measure. No rudeness was implied.

"I'm his uncle," Print added.

The spry man nodded, removed a toothpick from his mouth, and pointed to the corral. "Over there," the man replied.

Behind the fence of lodgepoles, lariats were flying through the air. Calves bawled amid the dust and smoke as they thudded to the ground. The men wrestled a bull calf to the ground while another man slit open its scrotum with a pocketknife, tossing warm testicles into a wooden bucket. One gland missed the bucket and instantly a thin cattle dog snapped up the warm morsel. The branding iron bit into the thick hair and hide. Smoke billowed and another "new" steer struggled to its feet, its backside still smoking. A big bull calf threw himself against the poles, trying to escape. Once. Twice. The third time, he landed on the top pole, snapping it and two more. He somersaulted over, landing on his back. He scrambled and was off before the cowhands could clear the broken fence.

With a slight squeeze of his legs, Print had the big chestnut off in a shot. In one fluid motion, Print uncoiled his riata, played out a loop, and tossed it around the bull calf's hind legs. He dallied up as Bob Tate set himself for the force and the calf hit the end of the rope. Horse and rider took the impact as Print sat deep in the saddle. The calf hung suspended in the air for a moment, then hit the ground. The big cow pony backed up just enough to keep the tension on the rope.

Several hands scrambled over the breached corral, heading for the struggling calf. One of them stopped and looked up at Print.

"Uncle Print?" he asked.

He turned to the spry man who had followed Print.

"This is my uncle, Print Ritter. ... Prentice Ritter."

Print and the spry man exchanged nods. Tom loosened the rope around the calf's hind legs as the other hands took over. His shirt was mottled with sweat and dust. Tom was lean and, like most of the Ritter clan, had bright red hair.

"What brings you out here? Thought maybe you'd died."

Print smiled slightly at the notion. "No, son, not yet. But your ma did. She passed away."

Tom said nothing. Neither did his face as he coiled another loop of the rope. "Did she say anything?" he asked.

"No, son. Her hired man found her in the vegetable garden," replied Print.

"Is he looking after the place?"

Print sighed. His wrists crossed over the horn of the saddle. "He is ... I need ta say something straight out: she wrote a will." Print tugged at the glove on his left hand. He looked straight into the face of his nephew. "She left it all to me."

He raised his gaze momentarily, watching the

cowhands wrestle the bull calf back over the broken opening. Then he looked back at the silent young man. "I don't know what was cros't between you two, but she done it. The land, the livestock, ever'thing. It ain't a fortune, but it's legit."

Print released his end of the rope from the horn and let it slip away.

"That's it?" Tom asked, his face as lifeless as his departed mother's.

Print reached inside his coat and removed an envelope, offering it to his nephew. "She did leave this for ya."

Tom stepped forward, took the envelope, looked at it, and stuffed it unopened into his shirt pocket. The two men looked at one another. Tom coiled up the last of the rope.

"I don't feel good about this, Nephew, not at all. I always figgered that it would all go ta you."

Tom tapped the coiled rope against his chaps. Print continued.

"That's why I come out here. I wanted to talk. Ya see, your mother made me the executor to her estate. That means I have to carry out the orders of her will. She left ever'thin' ta me, 'cept there was a codicil. You can buy the old Fairbairn place—the three sections that run down from Steens to the Mahluer from her estate—if ya've a mind to."

"I can buy it?" Tom asked.

Print nodded. "Market price."

A bitter Tom turned to walk away.

"Will's on file over ta Burns'," Print called after him.

Tom stopped and turned to face his uncle. "Sonnuva bitch. That's mother's milk for ya."

Print nodded in agreement. "More like hind tit, son."

Tom looked over at the spry man and then back to Print. "Any more good news for me, Uncle?"

Print shifted in the saddle. "Look, son, I don't like this any mor'n you do, but I got this idea … might work out for both of us ... maybe. I got this idea ta take horses back to Wyoming."

Print extracted a newspaper clipping from his coat pocket. "Listen ta this: Wanted: Hot- or cold-blooded horses. Sound and disease free. Three to eight years of age. Proof of ownership required. Purchase price commiserate with the quality of stock. Contact William or Malcolm Moncrieffe, Quarter Circle A Ranch, Sheridan, Wyoming— Agents for Her Majesty's War Office, British Empire."

Print looked up from the paper to gauge Tom's reaction. He continued. "Why don't we take some of yer ma's money an' buy a big string of horses? Might be a handy way ta increase our capital."

"You mean your capital. They ain't got horses in Wyoming?"

A vexed Print pursed his lips. "Try not ta get all swolled up an' just think about this fer a minute. A fella name of Haythorne was out this way last year. Tried ta hire me to help drive a herd of five hundr'd head back ta Valentine, Nebraska. He had a contract with the Indian Agency ta supply horses for the Rosebud Reservation—"

"How many? An' what kind?" Tom interrupted.

Now yer gettin' it, Print thought. "I figger we could handle easy five hundr'd, maybe more if we took on a couple a boys. I'm thinkin' tough, high desert mustangs. Easy keepers. They kin go unshod and oughta be fairly broke by the time we get ta Sheridan."

Print could see that Tom wasn't as sold as he had hoped.

"An' you think I should quit here an' help make you richer than my ma already has?" Tom asked, looking over at the spry man and then back to his uncle.

"That's not my intention."

"We'd do this on shares?" Tom asked.

Print nodded. "I figger fifty/fifty split on the profits after expenses and loan repayment."

"Loan repayment?"

Print shifted again and Bob Tate responded by shifting his weight from one hind leg to the other. "That's right, loan repayment, ta the bank. I'd hafta put the ranch up as collateral."

"What the hell kinda deal is that? Yer gonna hock the family place to buy horses?"

Print was beginning to lose patience. "Well, that's one way a lookin' at it."

"What's the other?" asked Tom.

"No disrespect meant, but ain't you spent enough time cuttin' the nuts off another man's cows for chuck an' wages?" replied Print, first looking at the spry man and then to Tom.

Print continued. "Keep it up an' you'll be walkin' aroun' like a crab, all stove up along with all the other bachelor cowhands from here to the Dalles—no disrespect meant."

Tom walked away. Print dismounted, flipped the stirrup over the saddle seat, and loosened the cinch strap. He lifted the saddle and moved the saddle blanket forward. Tom turned and walked back to his uncle.

"Here," he said, handing him the coiled riata.

Print took the rope and his eyes followed Tom as he walked around to the off side of the horse. Tom stared across the seat of the saddle at his uncle.

"Still ridin' old Bob Tate, I see."

Print smiled. "You bet," he replied.

Tom turned to the spry man, who nodded and took the toothpick from his mouth and pointed to the bunkhouse. Tom looked back at Print and said, "I'll get my stuff."

Having reset the blanket and saddle properly, Print tightened the cinch strap, dropped the stirrup back down, and said to the spry man, "Guess I'm gonna leave you a man short."

The spry man stuck the toothpick back in his mouth.

"Tom's a hell of a hand. Hope things work out for you two."

Soon Tom returned with two horses, one saddled and the other with a packsaddle and his gear. He swung into the saddle.

"Maybe we'll see ya next spring," Print said to the spry man.

The spry man nodded and replied, "Keep yer nose to the wind, 'specially in that Green River country. There's desperate citizens that populate that land."

The two men turned their mounts and started off. The sun was now high, reminding Print that he hadn't had any coffee this day.

CHAPTER TWO

The following month Print and Tom spent going from ranch to ranch buying horses. They ranged from as far south as the 3 Mile Ranch at the bottom end of the Steens to the Juniper place, then back over to Barton Lake, where they put up their stock in the big round barn that Peter French had built back in the early eighties, which was the talk of the countryside. After a lifetime of "excitement," Print found he still had a curiosity about things, even if it was only what the next week might bring.

They were sorting through some of the stock at French's barn. Print pointed to a red roan colt that Tom had picked out from stock over at the Venator Ranch that was penned up in the stone corral. "How rode out is that one?"

Tom shrugged. "He ain't no Bob Tate, but he'll do," he replied.

Print tossed a loop over the colt's head. He didn't fight and stood quietly as Print saddled him and slipped on a hackamore. In a side pen were four cows that they had picked up along the way and were planning on leaving there. Print said they would let the owners over at Ruby's know about them when they passed through.

Print quietly swung up and then carefully settled in the saddle. The cow pony stood stock-still. He then walked over to the pen with the strays in it. He opened the gate from atop the horse, passed through, and closed it from behind. At the far end of the pen, the strays bunched up.

Tom took a seat on the wall of the stone corral to watch. Print approached the strays, moving in on a white-faced cow. The bunch broke and the pony cut right, splitting the cows. The half with the white-faced cow darted off to the side and then doubled back to the far end. Print and the pony were right on them. Two jumps and the pony had "whitey" separated. When the cow tried to bolt, the pony jumped right up and cut him off. Then he'd ease off to give the cow time to think it out. As soon as the cow moved, the pony was on him. No matter which way it turned, the pony would sweep left or right. Finally, the cow gave up and shut it down. Print wheeled the red roan and trotted over to Tom. He stopped and rested his crossed arms on the horn.

"Yer right. He ain't no Bob Tate," he said, smiling. "But he'll do."

They camped in the stone corral that was really a long chute entrance to the round barn. They stayed up late that night and Print told his nephew stories of the vaqueros who had broken horses under that round roof. And of horses that had broken some men.

They mustered their growing herd at the Hanleys' Bella A Ranch and headed west to Wagontire Mountain and Bill Brown's place. "Wagontire" Brown raised horses and sheep. He was hard on his help and spent long periods having to run his place on his own. He wrote his checks on wrapping paper and the bank in Burns accepted every one of them for almost forty years. He tended his flocks out in the bush and lived on nuts and raisins with a pinch of strychnine. "Just enough to kill the appetite, not the cook." He raised exactly the kind of horses Print wanted and needed.

When they had ganged over five hundred head, Print took off for Canyon City and John Day and then back to Burns, taking care of the paperwork, finances, and provisions.

Early on the morning of the fifteenth of May, with four extra men to help get them started, Print and Tom emptied the pens to head for the Moncrieffe brothers' in Sheridan.

"Let's wheel 'em to the right!" yelled Print.

Slowly, the milling horses started in a counterclockwise direction, shoving and bumping, some rearing onto the backs of others. The men did a good job keeping them turned in. Clouds of dust rose, obscuring the men and the herd. From high up where the geese flew, it must have looked like a giant turning mandala.

Print rode around the herd counter to its movement. His blood was up. It pumped through him, and he didn't feel any aches. He felt strong. He wasn't thinking about making money or bank loans or squaring things with his nephew. He rode in close on the turning horses, close enough that they bumped his leg. It may have looked like mayhem, but he controlled it. He felt solid. And young again, or at least younger. He pulled the kerchief down that covered his face.

"Let 'em go! Let 'em go! Head 'em east an' let 'em go!"

The men eased off, and as they did, the circle expanded until the lead mares broke free and more or less headed off to the east. The circle undid itself. Once the herd straightened out, all the boys had to do was keep up on either side. One man with the packhorses brought up the rear far behind. Five hundred and thirty-six horses charged into the rays of the morning sun.

CHAPTER THREE

The clipper ship plowed down the deep troughs and then through the cresting waves of the South China Sea. The captain stood behind the helmsman on the shifting quarterdeck. Spray from the waves breaking over the bowsprit soaked everything topside. The captain grabbed the rail of the quarterdeck as the ship laid heavy to port and slid down the lee side of a huge wave. All her sails were reefed save one spritsail to help her keep her heading. The helmsman struggled with the great wheel. The captain stepped forward to help him. Together they headed her almost directly into the wind. As she crested the next wave, her bow all the way to the keel came out of the water. Then down she plunged, thrusting her nose into the gray-green ocean covering her fo'c'sle.

"Good God, man, keep her inta the wind, man!" the captain screamed. "It's gunna be an ugly night. I'm going below!" he yelled to the sailor.

He noticed that the wind was rising as it caught the tops of the waves and skimmed spray off them. He opened the hatch and descended the ladder, sliding the hatch cover closed behind him.

"Bagwell! Bagwell!" the captain shouted.

From the darkened companionway, the first mate appeared, his slicker already in hand.

"I want you topside at the wheel. Take two men to help. She's gonna have her teeth in us tonight."

"Aye, aye, capt'n," he replied.

"An' get all hands going on the bilge pumps, port an' starboard."

"Aye, capt'n," answered the mate, slipping on his foul-weather gear.

The captain made his way forward along the companionway until he got to the next opening and descended the ladder to the next deck. Then he reversed himself, heading aft along that deck's companionway to the next opening, and braced himself against the bulkhead as the ship rose up and hove to port. He could hear the transom groan as the sea pressed on all sides. At the bottom of the ladder, a lantern swung, barely lighting the hold. With all the portholes and air shafts secured for the gale, the stench in the compartment was retching. Even with a lifetime at sea behind him, the captain gagged as he took the lantern down and made his way forward.

The captain had a flinty face and a flinty heart. He held the lamp high as he walked to the motion of the ship. Secured to the ship's bulkheads were large containers with bolted doors and barred windows. He held the light to one of the windows and leaned close, bracing himself as the ship rolled to port. The swaying lamp revealed young Chinese girls huddled together. Some so overcome with sickness from the storm lay on the floor of the container, exhausted from retching. The wooden bucket used as a toilet had overturned in the storm and its contents sloshed back and forth. He looked into all the lashed containers and then returned the lantern to its hook and doused the light. He ascended the ladder, wondering how much the storm would affect his calculated arrival date in San Francisco.

CHAPTER FOUR

After a couple of miles, the herd had thinned out and was now a long stretched-out line. The pace had slacked off some, so the riders urged them on. Print wanted to make sure the herd understood that slowing down or stopping was always going to be his idea, not theirs. They ran along the East Fork for a half an hour with a stout, flea-bitten gray mare in the lead. Tom rode close to the front of the herd, watching the mare. He had already decided she wasn't going to be sold in Sheridan. He was keeping her for himself. As she crested an incline, she eased into a trot, and Tom did the same. Soon all of the herd was at the trot.

Print rode up to Tom. He was glad to see that his nephew was taking to sharing the decision making already. Tom nodded to him as Bob Tate pulled alongside.

"Nothin' like a five-mile romp ta knock the edge off 'em!" yelled a smiling Print.

Tom nodded and pushed his horse just a little ahead of his uncle's big chestnut. Print responded by pulling up even to Tom.

"Figger out who's gonna be the caporal of this mob?"

Tom pointed to the lead horse churning out in front. "That gray mare!" he yelled. "Maybe the piebald next to her. Either one."

Print nodded at Tom's assessment. "You can ease up a bit, but let's keep 'em moving. We'll water 'em at the north end of the lake. I want 'em good an' tired when we make camp tonight."

Print peeled off and headed back toward the rear of the herd, checking with the outriders.

That afternoon the herd walked into a meadow on the north edge of Malheur Lake, tired and ready to graze. The men went about setting up camp for the night, while two stayed in the saddle, slowly walking around the herd, easing back in any that wanted to feed elsewhere.

Print had already tended to the packhorses and was busy cooking as the cowboys hauled their gear around the fire. It was still hours until sunset, but the day had worked up an appetite for both the herd and the men. Tom and another hand dropped a load of wood beside the cook fire for Print.

"Hope you boys are hungry. Thought I'd do 'er up a little special tonight. Figger this'll be the last company we'll have for a while."

The coffeepot was passed around. A pot of beans bubbled beside the fire, and set in a ring of coals off to the side was a Dutch oven. A big skillet filled with beefsteaks sputtered as Print sliced an onion and sprinkled the rings over the steaks.

"Trick to makin' a good pot a beans is a quarter stick of Mexican vanilla, a big slug of blackstrap molasses, an' a strong jolt of bug juice," said Print as he stirred the pot. He lifted the wooden spoon, licked it, and then stirred the pot again.

He stood up and looked to the south. A creek where the horses watered ran into a marsh and beyond that was the lake. Snowy egrets and cranes stalked about in the salt grass. Hundreds of terns would take flight and then immediately drop down again as another flock would take off and then land. Pintails wheeled in the sky overhead, and way out on the lake a vee of Canada geese crossed over. Beyond that lay the Steens, their ridgelines and crevices white with snow. He reached down and tossed a couple of pieces of old juniper on the fire. With a long fork, he flipped the steaks as the wood caught fire and popped.

The men sidled up to the fire with tin plates and forks in hand.

"Looks like first-rate grub tonight, Mr. Ritter," said one of the hands.

"Boys, the culinary procedures I have implemented tonight do not fall under the category of 'grub.' Nor 'chuck,' for that matter. No, sir," replied Print.

Using his wadded-up kerchief, he pulled the Dutch oven from the coals and removed the lid to reveal big, puffy brown biscuits. With the long fork, he slapped grilled steaks onto each man's plate as they helped themselves to beans and biscuits. Print wadded up the bloody, brown paper that the meat had been in and tossed it into the fire.

The camp grew silent save the clinking of forks on tin plates as Tom approached.

"Grab a plate, son," said Print. "Havin' beefsteak for supper will be few an' far between on this trip."

Tom took a plate and fork and helped himself. "I hobbled those lead mares. I think they're all tired enough, but we might as well take advantage of the extra help tonight to watch over 'em," said Tom, piling beans over his steak.

He sat down and took out his large pocketknife to cut up his steak. Print poured drippings from the skillet into his plate and hooked crispy onion rings onto the big fork. He sat down and sopped up the drippings with a biscuit, ate the onion rings, and licked his fingers.

"Boys, we'll be passin' north of the Circle Bar 'bout noon tomorrow. Guess that's the best jumpin' off spot for you," said Print, popping the last of the greasy biscuit into his mouth.

"Mr. Ritter, would ya mind if Bob an' I skinned outta here after supper? We'd like to pull for the ranch tonight, if ya don't mind," said a tall, towheaded lad.

Print looked at them and then smiled. "Guess not, boys. Can't be you're in a hurry to catch up on yer chores?"

"No, sir," smiled the lad.

"Couldn't be there's some pretty felines in Princeton needin' attention? Well, be careful boys. ... Remember what happen'd ta Adam at the apple sale."

"Yes, sir."

"I'll get you yer wages," said Print.

"That's all right, Mr. Ritter, you can settle up with Pete. He'll get it to us."

"You boys are in a sweat. Good enough. Thanks fer the help."

"See ya in the fall, Mr. Ritter."

Print nodded and touched the brim of his hat. He turned to the others. "A meal this fine oughta be that the cook don't hafta clean up. Gentlemen, it's all yours."

Print took out his penknife from a vest pocket and a piece of wood to whittle on. Soon the camp settled down. The fire was fed. Overhead was the sound of snipes in flight, and out on the lake a trumpeter swan called out in the dark.

"Lonely drake out there," said Print to Tom.

Tom nodded.

"Not bad for the first day."

"For the first day," added Tom.

A breakfast of leftover beans and coffee and the men had the horses on the move as light was just seeping into the eastern sky. By noon they had gotten the herd to just north of the Circle Bar Ranch. As they approached, they saw a lone figure mounted and waiting for them in the brush. Tom brought the herd to a stop and, with Print, rode over to the waiting rider.

He was turned out like much of the rest of the hands, still wearing his winter woollies chaps. He looked pale and raised his hand to motion them to stop when they got close to him.

"Morning," said the young man.

"Not much of it left," said Print.

"Name's Billy Via. I thought ya might be looking for help."

"Well, Billy Via, I'm Print Ritter, and this is my nephew, Tom. We're not local. We're headin' ta Wyoming and we're not takin' on any hands at this time."

"Yes, sir, I know. Bub Waters told me. They came in late last night … from Princeton."

"No worse for the wear?" asked Print.

"No, sir."

"Sorry we can't help ya, son. We're workin' on a kinda tight purse on this deal," said Print.

"I understand, sir, but I won't cost ya much. I could really use the job, sir."

"You in trouble?" asked Tom.

Tom and Print waited.

"Not exactly. … See, I had a pretty bad wreck a couple years back. A bad'n went up an' over on me. Busted my appendix. Doctor got that taken care of, but my gut was torn and he couldn't stitch 'er, so he left a hole."

"A hole?" asked Tom.

"Yes, sir. Thing is, it never really healed up."

Again the men waited in silence.

"It never did sort itself out an' now it just leaks."

"Leaks?"

"Yes, sir. It leaks."

"What's it leak?" asked Tom.

"Shit, mostly, sir."

"Shit?"

"Yes, sir. Mostly."

"I really don't see how we can help ya, son. We ain't doctors," said Print.

"No, sir. I don't need a doctor. I got it under control. I keep it covered an' change the towels regular. I am clean in all my habits, sir. My problem is the smell, sir."

"The smell?"

"Yes, sir. It's a heinous odor to it. Ungodly, really. I'm used to it, but it is hard on others. Can't hold a job being anywhere 'round other hands. Not even sleepin' out in the barn."

Tom shifted his weight in the saddle and looked at Print. It was all they could do to keep from grinning.

"Well, we ain't deprived in the smelling department either, son," said Print.

Billy looked away and then back at them. "No, sir. I know that, but I figgered an outdoor job like this might work out okay. I'll stay off by myself. Make my own camp away from you. Tend ta myself. I'll stay downwind of ya. I can handle horses with the best of 'em. Ask the boys. They ain't got it in fer me, they just can't stand the smell."

Print looked at Tom for his thoughts and then at Billy. "I don't know, son. I'd like ta help, but I just don't know … "

"I'm about at the end of my string, sir. I'll make it work for ya."

"An' if it don't?" asked Tom.

"You'll get no argument from me. I'll move on."

"Just like that?" asked Tom.

"Yes, sir. Just like that."

Tom turned to Print. "Your call, Uncle."

Print brushed his moustache with his finger. "Okay, Billy Via, we'll try it out for a while. Come on."

The young man grinned and got some color back in his face.

"I'll just stay here 'til you've settled up with the boys."

Print and Tom turned their horses back to the waiting herd.

"Yes, yes," the eager woman replied.

She waved two old hags over to her and pointed out the girls. The old women sat one of the naked girls on a chair and spread her legs apart. She poked and prodded and peered about the young girl's crotch. She nodded and another girl was seated. When the fourth girl was inspected, the crouching old woman said something to the seller and the girl was yanked away.

"No virgin. No sale. You pick," she said. "What about lucky girl?"

The woman dragged the girl to the chair and sat her down. The girl had seen what had happened to the other girls and still she struggled. All three of the older women slapped and hit her about the face and head. The frantic seller growled something at the girl. The girl reluctantly complied. The women checked her carefully and nodded yes.

The seller tried to compose herself as she turned to the man, who was thoroughly enjoying the medical exam.

"She make much moneys for you."

"I'm not sure."

"Oh, yes. Lucky girl for you. I give you very good price."

The man smiled. His mouth was full of rotten yellow teeth.

The woman reached inside the folds of her robe and pulled out a small leather flask. She pantomimed opening it and tipping its mouth on her forefinger. She turned to the "lucky girl" and opened the front of her pajamas. The girl struggled; her pants were still around her ankles. The woman grabbed the left breast of the young girl, squeezing it hard. Tears of pain came to her eyes. With gritted teeth, the woman mimed rubbing the flask's contents on the girl's nipple.

"Good time, boy. Kiss, kiss. Love, love lucky girl."

The man stared at her.

"Good time, boy, kiss, kiss," she said.

"What if the wind changes in the night?" asked Tom.

Print chuckled. As they approached, the men gathered around them. "Guess it's time to pay you, boys."

"Yer gonna have yer hands full, Mr. Ritter. Sure ya don't want us to go along? At least for a few days?" asked the rangy cowboy.

"I think we got a handle on it, boys. 'Sides, I just took on a man."

"Billy Via?" asked the cowboy.

Print and Tom both looked over their shoulder at the young man on his horse where they had left him. They turned back to the cowboy.

"He's a good hand, but … "

"But … ? Ya mean the smell?" asked Tom.

"Sir, it's like dummy foals. There's some things that just wasn't intended to live. I'd say Billy's one of 'em."

Print looked at the man for a long moment. "We'll see."

CHAPTER FIVE

The figure stopped in front of Old Saint Mary's to strike a match. He lit the cheroot and puffed as the church bells rang out the hour. The heavy fog that had rolled in seemed to flatten the pealing of the church's bells. He puffed again and looked up at the cathedral's facade.

By the light of the street lamp, he read the words chiseled over the entryway: SON, OBSERVE THE TIME … AND FLY FROM EVIL. He flicked out the match, took another puff, and turned up the frayed collar on his coat. Another figure, much shorter, came up to him from behind. The smaller man stopped only momentarily and then seemed to glide across the street. The first man stepped off the curb and crossed Grant Avenue, following the little man. He disappeared into the fog and the darkness. He could hear the clanking of the streetcar over on Powell Street. It was all he could do to keep sight of the little specter. At one point it stopped, waiting, and then moved on, heading for Chinatown.

He could smell the cooking from the Asian quarter. It masked the tainted air of Chinatown. The little specter stopped again, waiting, then ducked into an alley that led to another. He turned the last corner and heard a knocking sound. A door opened, and a light shone on the little Chinaman who had brought him there. He entered, then turned to see his guide slip away. Two Chinamen motioned him to follow them down a hallway that led to a door behind which stairs descended to a large room.

The room was filled with Asiatics. There was a line of

shivering, naked girls in the process of being scrubbed by several old women. The steamy of lye soap. Other women were dressing girls chattering as they outfitted the young women shuffled over to the visitor.

"You come to buy?" she asked.

"I have," he replied.

"Good, good. You got money, I got girls."

"I got money."

"How many you want?"

"Five," he said, raising his hand with spread

"Good. Any you want?"

"Five virgins. Virgins. Guaranteed. Five. You stand?"

The woman nodded. "No problem. Can do. gins. You pick."

He stepped forward, inspecting the girls who dripping and frightened. If they turned away or c themselves, he would jerk them around to stand and

"I'll take this one … and her." He pulled the the wash line. He turned to the girls who were dre opened the front of their pajamas one at a time. Or clutched her robe and he slapped her hard across th The woman who was
selling stepped between them and slapped the girl e harder. The woman opened the front of the girl's paj

"You like?"

"She's a virgin?" he asked.

"Absolute. Absolute virgin. You like? Pretty girl. make you much money. You like?"

"Maybe."

"You like her. I know. I make you good price. Sh lucky girl. Make you lucky man."

He moved on, picking three more girls. "All virgi You guarantee."

"What if the wind changes in the night?" asked Tom.

Print chuckled. As they approached, the men gathered around them. "Guess it's time to pay you, boys."

"Yer gonna have yer hands full, Mr. Ritter. Sure ya don't want us to go along? At least for a few days?" asked the rangy cowboy.

"I think we got a handle on it, boys. 'Sides, I just took on a man."

"Billy Via?" asked the cowboy.

Print and Tom both looked over their shoulder at the young man on his horse where they had left him. They turned back to the cowboy.

"He's a good hand, but … "

"But … ? Ya mean the smell?" asked Tom.

"Sir, it's like dummy foals. There's some things that just wasn't intended to live. I'd say Billy's one of 'em."

Print looked at the man for a long moment. "We'll see."

CHAPTER FIVE

The figure stopped in front of Old Saint Mary's to strike a match. He lit the cheroot and puffed as the church bells rang out the hour. The heavy fog that had rolled in seemed to flatten the pealing of the church's bells. He puffed again and looked up at the cathedral's facade.

By the light of the street lamp, he read the words chiseled over the entryway: SON, OBSERVE THE TIME … AND FLY FROM EVIL. He flicked out the match, took another puff, and turned up the frayed collar on his coat. Another figure, much shorter, came up to him from behind. The smaller man stopped only momentarily and then seemed to glide across the street. The first man stepped off the curb and crossed Grant Avenue, following the little man. He disappeared into the fog and the darkness. He could hear the clanking of the streetcar over on Powell Street. It was all he could do to keep sight of the little specter. At one point it stopped, waiting, and then moved on, heading for Chinatown.

He could smell the cooking from the Asian quarter. It masked the tainted air of Chinatown. The little specter stopped again, waiting, then ducked into an alley that led to another. He turned the last corner and heard a knocking sound. A door opened, and a light shone on the little Chinaman who had brought him there. He entered, then turned to see his guide slip away. Two Chinamen motioned him to follow them down a hallway that led to a door behind which stairs descended to a large room.

The room was filled with Asiatics. There was a line of

shivering, naked girls in the process of being washed and scrubbed by several old women. The steamy room smelled of lye soap. Other women were dressing girls, scolding and chattering as they outfitted the young women. A woman shuffled over to the visitor.

"You come to buy?" she asked.

"I have," he replied.

"Good, good. You got money, I got girls."

"I got money."

"How many you want?"

"Five," he said, raising his hand with spread fingers.

"Good. Any you want?"

"Five virgins. Virgins. Guaranteed. Five. You understand?"

The woman nodded. "No problem. Can do. Five virgins. You pick."

He stepped forward, inspecting the girls who cowered, dripping and frightened. If they turned away or covered themselves, he would jerk them around to stand and face him.

"I'll take this one … and her." He pulled them out of the wash line. He turned to the girls who were dressed. He opened the front of their pajamas one at a time. One girl clutched her robe and he slapped her hard across the face. The woman who was selling stepped between them and slapped the girl even harder. The woman opened the front of the girl's pajamas.

"You like?"

"She's a virgin?" he asked.

"Absolute. Absolute virgin. You like? Pretty girl. She make you much money. You like?"

"Maybe."

"You like her. I know. I make you good price. She lucky girl. Make you lucky man."

He moved on, picking three more girls. "All virgins. You guarantee."

"Yes, yes," the eager woman replied.

She waved two old hags over to her and pointed out the girls. The old women sat one of the naked girls on a chair and spread her legs apart. She poked and prodded and peered about the young girl's crotch. She nodded and another girl was seated. When the fourth girl was inspected, the crouching old woman said something to the seller and the girl was yanked away.

"No virgin. No sale. You pick," she said. "What about lucky girl?"

The woman dragged the girl to the chair and sat her down. The girl had seen what had happened to the other girls and still she struggled. All three of the older women slapped and hit her about the face and head. The frantic seller growled something at the girl. The girl reluctantly complied. The women checked her carefully and nodded yes.

The seller tried to compose herself as she turned to the man, who was thoroughly enjoying the medical exam.

"She make much moneys for you."

"I'm not sure."

"Oh, yes. Lucky girl for you. I give you very good price."

The man smiled. His mouth was full of rotten yellow teeth.

The woman reached inside the folds of her robe and pulled out a small leather flask. She pantomimed opening it and tipping its mouth on her forefinger. She turned to the "lucky girl" and opened the front of her pajamas. The girl struggled; her pants were still around her ankles. The woman grabbed the left breast of the young girl, squeezing it hard. Tears of pain came to her eyes. With gritted teeth, the woman mimed rubbing the flask's contents on the girl's nipple.

"Good time, boy. Kiss, kiss. Love, love lucky girl."

The man stared at her.

"Good time, boy, kiss, kiss," she said.